jumped over
THREE POTS
AND A PAN

and landed **SMACK**

in the garbage can!

WRITTEN BY

PAMELA JANE

ILLUSTRATED BY

HINA IMTIAZ

SchifferKids™

4880 Lower Valley Road, Atglen, PA 19310

At camp, big **A** was on kitchen patrol when **B** jumped over a mixing bowl.

I bet I jump even farther than you."

Then C leaped over
three pots and a pan -

and
landed smack
in the
garbage
can!

"Good grief," he said,
"this is terrible luck.

C kicked and wiggled
and let out a shout,

"Hey, someone help me,
I can't get out!"

They looked all over,
but no one could see

the slightest sign of
old three-armed E.

"It's terribly spooky,"
N muttered to **Q**,
"For **O**, **P**, and **R**
have disappeared, too."

Then **S** leaned over and whispered to **T**, "Oh my, an alphabet mystery!"

Four letters had
vanished without a trace,
but it was **U** who
cracked the case.

Just then - surprise! -
from behind a tree
out jumped four letters
- R, O, P, and E.

"For C jumped over
three pots and a pan
and landed smack in
the garbage can."

And so four letters,
R, O, P, and **E,**

teamed up to save
the unfortunate **C.**

A ROPE, some friends,
and a fabulous plan
all rescued C from
the garbage can!

❤ TO ARIA WITH LOVE ❤

TYPE SET IN DRUNK FONT/ NICKNAME/ KGSECONDCHANCES SOLID/ BORDEN

ISBN: 978-0-7643-5795-4 (HARD COVER)
ISBN: 978-0-7643-5877-7 (SOFT COVER)
PRINTED IN CHINA

PUBLISHED BY SCHIFFER KIDS
AN IMPRINT OF SCHIFFER PUBLISHING, LTD.
4880 LOWER VALLEY ROAD
ATGLEN, PA 19310
PHONE: (610) 593-1777; FAX: (610) 593-2002
E-MAIL: INFO@SCHIFFERBOOKS.COM
WEB: WWW.SCHIFFERBOOKS.COM

FOR OUR COMPLETE SELECTION OF FINE BOOKS ON THIS AND RELATED SUBJECTS, PLEASE VISIT OUR WEBSITE AT WWW.SCHIFFERBOOKS.COM. YOU MAY ALSO WRITE FOR A FREE CATALOG.

SCHIFFER PUBLISHING'S TITLES ARE AVAILABLE AT SPECIAL DISCOUNTS FOR BULK PURCHASES FOR SALES PROMOTIONS OR PREMIUMS. SPECIAL EDITIONS, INCLUDING PERSONALIZED COVERS, CORPORATE IMPRINTS, AND EXCERPTS, CAN BE CREATED IN LARGE QUANTITIES FOR SPECIAL NEEDS. FOR MORE INFORMATION, CONTACT THE PUBLISHER.

WE ARE ALWAYS LOOKING FOR PEOPLE TO WRITE BOOKS ON NEW AND RELATED SUBJECTS. IF YOU HAVE AN IDEA FOR A BOOK, PLEASE CONTACT US AT PROPOSALS@SCHIFFERBOOKS.COM.